The Adventures of Sir George the Wise Knight and Scraggin Dragon

The Quest

By Valeria Vata Rae
Illustrated by Christopher
Aaron Barbee

may
Sir
George
+
Scraggin
Dragon
be
with
you
on all
Your
adventures!
Valeria

Dedicated to our mom who loved a good
adventure.

First edition
Text copyright © by Valeria Vata Rae
Illustrations by Christopher Aaron Barbee
copyright © Valeria Vata Rae

Self-Published via Createspace
A division of Amazon   March 2017
ISBN-13   978-1544093239
ISBN-10   1544093233

CONTENTS

Acknowledgements

I would like to acknowledge Sir Terence Pratchett for his amazing imagination and keen social perception that have inspired me for many years. Also I am grateful to all those who have traveled in the realms of dragons and shared their experience, and for the dragons who have brought so much magic into my life. I could not have completed this book without the support and talent of my brother Christopher, and I would like to thank Judy Crawford, my eagle eyed editor. Lastly, I am indebted to Abraham-Hicks my spiritual teachers.

Chapter 1

The Quest

Have you ever met a dragon, an actual dragon? Dragons are said to be big, scaly and very dangerous. So when George, a young knight, sets off to find a dragon that was said to be terrorizing the land, he was shaking in his boots!

George was tall, fair skinned, with brown eyes and reddish brown hair. That morning he pulled on his chain mail and fastened the straps of his polished suit of armor. He hefted his sword and looked at his shield. It was pounded steel in the chevron shape of his family's crest, and on it was painted a black dragon. Will it protect me? He wondered.

He had packed his saddle bags with a pair of warm woolen leggings, his long black tunic, extra socks, his knife, a writing satchel and the tinderbox the blacksmith had given him. Around his neck he hung his lucky rabbit's foot and tucked it inside his armor. Next he slid the heavy metal helmet on his head. With the visor up, George looked at himself in the mirror. He had just turned 18 and although he had started knight training when he was just 10 and had worn this armor many times before, the image that looked back at him did not seem familiar. George was no longer a boy, and not yet not a man. He wondered what he would see in his reflection when he returned, if he returned.

As George descended the grand stone staircase, the ring of his boots echoed throughout the empty hall. Everyone was outside. He could hear their voices and laughter, and he could feel their excitement. This was an important day for them too.

The court yard was alive with a festive spirit. Brightly colored pennants and banners hung from the walls. Everyone wore their best garments. The groom was waiting with George's horse, Nesset, a big black stallion. All the folks from the village and the castle family had come to wish him well, and to see him off on his quest. They smiled and waved as he stepped out of the door. He heard someone call out, "That's our brave lad, dragon slayer, we are so proud of you!"

But his mother, father and little sister did not look so happy. They could not hide their fear. There were so many stories about brave knights who had gone to face the dragon and had never returned. They did not want George to be one of those. George's mother had tears in her eyes, and his sister hid her face in her mother's skirts so that her brother could not see her crying. George's father, Lord Aarrun ruler of the realm, put his hand on his son's strong shoulder and said, "You are brave, clever and well trained. If anyone can get the best of this beast, it will be you. Take good care, and bring yourself back to us!"

"I will Father." replied George.

George's face wore a look of determination. It did not betray his real feelings of excitement and fear. He wanted his family to have confidence in him. And he wanted to give the whole village a reason to be proud of him. The young knight was resolved to return with his own stories of how he faced the monstrous dragon and had won!

As George threw his pack behind the saddle and mounted, Magda the cook came running out of the castle kitchen with a big sack which she had filled with biscuits, cheese, apples and figs. She too was crying. As she handed up the sack, she patted George on the leg and smiled through her tears. "Come back soon." she whispered. George nodded to her, and then scanned the crowd to find the familiar face of Lucinda, the miller's daughter. She was standing at the back of the crowd and George could tell she had been crying also. He nodded to her.

With a long last look at those he loved, George turned his horse toward the gate and started off on his quest. As Nesset's big hooves sounded across the draw bridge, George saw the farmers in the field stop their work and wave to him. He waved back. Yes, he was really on his way. He took a deep breath, kicked his horse into a trot, and headed toward the far Black Mountains.

As George followed the road through the field, he gazed at the farm land around the castle. It was mid-summer, and the grain was tall and ripening to a rich golden color. It would be cut soon, the grain beaten from the stalks and put into large sacks. The farmers would load the grain onto carts and haul it to the castle. There it would be ground beneath the big stone millwheel into flour. The flour was put back into the sacks and stacked in the corner until the farmers came to fetch them. Some of the flour was kept for the castle family to pay for the grinding.

George thought of all this as he rode along. He loved harvest time and the big festival that was held at the end of the thrashing. All the farmers and their families gathered in the castle. They built a huge bon fire in the court yard to dance around. Long tables were set up, decorated with flower garlands and covered with a great feast. Oh, the food! George's mouth watered just thinking about it. And then there was his friend Lucinda. She was tall for her age with very long black hair and laughing eyes. She liked to tease George by sneaking up on him, saying "Auuugggg!" while making an awful face. It never really scared George, but he pretended like it did to make her laugh. They had grown up together. Now he asked himself, will I ever see that smile again? Will we dance around the harvest fire together this fall? He shook his head, best not to think of that now, and he nudged Nesset into a gallop.

Chapter 2

Screemac

At the edge of the field, George turned onto the track that led into the forest. These were friendly woods where George had played with his friends as a young boy, and had gone hunting with his father. Deep green with sunlight streaking through the leaves, the birds sang high up in the branches. George felt safe here, but he had not been on this trail alone before. He could feel the fear of what lay ahead rising up in his mind.

The road curved as it went deeper into the forest and was covered with pine needles from the evergreen trees. Nesset's steps made no sound. In fact, George realized the bird song was gone as well. The eerie quiet made him uncomfortable. The only sound was his armor creaking and his heart pounding.

Then George heard a strange whistling up ahead. He reined Nesset to a stop and listened. George couldn't see anything. Slowly he pulled up his sword and shield from where they hung on his saddle and gently urged Nesset forward. In his imagination, he saw all sorts of frightful things, a huge giant carrying a club and a tiger with a mouthful of teeth. And then his imagination really got to work and showed him a snake with three heads!

He stopped and said out loud, "All right now, enough of that, for one thing we don't even have tigers in these woods and for another, if those monsters lived around here, I would have heard about it. So just knock it off imagination! Show me something I can deal with, something friendly and helpful."

At that moment, his mind revealed to him a gnome about three feet tall with a wide smile, a long white beard, and twinkling black eyes. George stared. This wasn't his imagination. There, standing on the path before him was indeed a gnome!

"Hi de ho!" he said, "what's a big man like you doin' in my wood?"

George was very surprised and a bit confused. He had never seen a gnome before except in picture books. Could this little fellow be real? He kept quiet.

The gnome spoke again, "So ye be a silent knight, eh? Ha ha ha!" he laughed heartily.

He sounds real enough, thought George, and in a voice as confident as he could muster he said, "I am Sir George of yonder castle, son of Lord Aarrun. And who might you be?"

The gnome hopped up on a stump next to the trail so that he was as tall as George and boomed, "I AM SCREEMAC, LORD OF THIS WOOD!" Then he laughed and laughed and fell down on the stump. He kicked his heels in the air and slapped his small hands on the wood.

George did not know what to think of this. He just stared at the little fellow until finally Screemac seemed to tire himself out from laughing and stood up.

Happily he said, "I be thanking ye sir, for that was the most fun I've had in ages!"

"Well, you are most welcome," said George a little suspiciously. He wondered if Screemac wasn't just a bit crazy in the head. Insanity, he knew, can be dangerous.

George decided that he had wasted enough time so he declared, "I must be going now, nice to have met you Screemac." He urged Nesset into a walk.

In a flash, the gnome jumped down on the trail in front of George. "Hold ye right there, my young knight." He said holding up both hands. "Ye be crossin' my wood, eh? If that be yer plan, ye'll be paying for the privilege."

George was beginning to feel annoyed. He knew all the land around the castle belonged to his father and said so.

To this Screemac shook his head. "Not this patch of wood." he declared. "This belongs to us, The Stynix. We have lived here for a thousand eons, and I am Screemac, Clan Leader." He declared with authority.

"So now," he said putting his hands on his hips, "ye be paying me what is due."

George asked, "And what would that be, pray tell?" his curiosity aroused.

"Well," Screemac once again leaped up on the stump, "do you have any tobacco on ye?" he asked hopefully.

"No," George said forcefully, "I don't smoke."

Screemac looked disappointed. "Aye, then, how about some of that fine mead they make at yon castle?"

George shook his head, "No, none of that either." George sighed, he was becoming impatient.

"I be takin' that sword then." declared the gnome.

"What?" George was outraged. He held his sword closer to his chest. "No you won't! My father had this made especially for me in the great forge."

"I see." replied the gnome with a sly grin. "Well, then ye can use that sword to do a deed for me and all me kin."

"What deed?" asked George, relaxing bit but still on his guard.

Screemac's face became serious. "We Stynix once had a grand place to live. It was in a cave that was cool in the summer, warm in the winter, and sheltered our whole clan. Last year a storm blew a great tree across the hole and we canna get in. You must chop up this tree and make a door for us!"

George did not see that he had much choice, so he nodded. "All right then," he sighed, "show me this irksome tree."

Chapter 3
The Tree

Screemac leaped down and bounded up the trail. George watched him in amazement. He didn't walk, or run, he hopped sort of like a rabbit.

George looked at his sword and thought, this sword was not meant to be used as an axe. He shook his head. I hope this doesn't take long. What am I anyway, a woodsman or a knight?

This brought to George's memory the day he became a knight. He was in the great hall of the castle kneeling before his father who touched his shoulder with the newly forged sword. The young knight recalled the pledge that he had repeated then, "I will do my best to protect those who seek protection, to help those in need, and to uphold the honor of my lord with courage, strength and wisdom." George thought, well, these wee folk are in need of help. I guess I am the one to do it. This may be a job for a knight after all.

They journeyed for nearly an hour through the darkening forest until they came to what appeared to be a large thistle bush next to the track. Screemac whistled loudly, and the thistle parted as if by magic. There was just enough room for George and his horse to pass through. Once they were on the other side, the bush closed up again.

Before them was a clearing. On the right lay a giant oak tree on its side. To the left, George saw only trees and undergrowth at first. Then he noticed movement under a berry bush. A Stynix was standing there so still that he blended into the bush. George became aware of many more of the wee folk standing, sitting on logs, peering down at him from up in tree branches. Their clothing matched the colors and shapes of the forest. George realized that The Stynix were very good at being invisible. No wonder they were not known to the folks in the castle.

Screemac jumped up on a large stone at the edge of the clearing and announced, "Welcome to our clan, Knight George. Here we stand awaiting your kindness." and then he laughed again and clapped his small hands.

George dismounted. He took off his helmet and set it on the rock next to Screemac. "So," he asked, "is that the troublesome tree?"

"That be he." said Screemac. "Can ye wield ye mighty sword and cut it away from our home cave? When the snow flies, we Stynix will be in sore misery if kept from it."

Taking his sword, George walked over to the tree. It was as big around as he was tall. He could see that it was lying up against a mound. Leaning his sword against the trunk, George climbed on top using branches for hand and foot holds. He looked down the other side. On one edge of the mound, he noticed the dirt had loosened and was beginning to fall into a hole.

He called to Screemac to hand up his sword, which the gnome did with a lot of huffing and puffing. George used it to poke into the space. Gradually the hole got bigger, and George could see into the cave. He worked down along the side of the trunk until he felt the metal of his sword hit something that sounded like stone. He called to Screemac who bounded up beside him.

"Look at this." George said.

Screemac exclaimed, "Ye he he, that be our home down there sure enough!"

George asked if the opening was big enough for the Stynix to use as an entrance. Screemac wiggled into the hole and dropped to the floor of the cave.

'Ye he he!" he cried and George could hear his gleeful laughter echoing back to him.

"Can you manage to build some steps on the inside?" George asked.

"No problem!" was the reply and soon Screemac's head appeared in the hole. He called to his fellows to assist him. Several Stynix detached themselves from the cover of the woods and ran to help. They barreled down the hole. George could hear a lot of grunting and moving about.

Finally Screemac climbed out with a happy shout, "He has done it! Knight George of yonder castle has reclaimed our home!" A loud cheer went up from the Stynix in the cave and from the surrounding woods. The whole clan now gathered around the trunk.

There must be a hundred of them, George thought happily, and he knew he had done a knightly good deed.

George used his sword to cut steps into the tree so that the Stynix could easily climb up to the new entrance. He stood on the ground watching them all scramble up and disappear into the cave.

Screemac smiled down at him. "Ye have helped those in need of helping, and we be grateful. Ye will always be welcome here." Then he threw a small leather pouch to George who opened it and found an old rusty key.

Puzzled, he looked at Screemac. "What is this?" he asked.

"Ye will know what it fits when ye finds the lock. Be safe and don't believe everything ye've been told!" He laughed again and was gone down into the cave.

George looked at the steps he had cut into the tree with satisfaction. Then he picked up his helmet from the rock and mounted Nesset. As they moved toward the thistle, it opened. He could just make out small feet shuffling under the bush and he heard a giggle.

Chapter 4

The Tinkling Wood

Back on the trail, George once again turned toward the east and continued along his way. It was getting dark and he knew he would need to find a place to rest for the night. Thick trees and brush hedged the trail on both side. Night fell and still George had not found a place to camp. The road was faintly lit by starlight, but the forest was black as the inside of a horse, as his father always said.

They walked on in silence. An owl hooted somewhere, again and again. George began to feel very uneasy. He had no idea what might live in these woods. The Stynix had been friendly enough, but then again he had never seen a gnome before that day. He gripped his sword tighter and drew up his shield. Even Nesset seemed on edge. His ears flicked this way and that.

George thought about his horse. His father had allowed him to choose a mount for himself from the castle stables when he was just 15. Nesset had been a three year old, tall and well-muscled, bred to carry a knight in full armor into battle. The young knight and his horse had trained to be warriors together, and had become best friends. George appreciated this now more than ever.

The moon appeared above the canopy bathing the trail in light. It revealed a clear place on the left. George reined into it. There was just enough room to tether Nesset and for him to stretch out. He took down his bedroll, which he carried on the back of his saddle, laid it out and leaned against a tree. His eyes watched the silver light on the trail. He thought, well, here I am where ever here is, and fell into a fitful sleep.

He woke to the gentle nudge of Nesset's nose against his cheek. Although it was morning, his little cove was still in shadow. He rose and took some of the cheese and fruit from his pack and ate quickly. Then drank from the water pouch he carried. "That will have to do." He said to Nesset. Mounting stiffly, he grunted, "And this is just the beginning."

His second day proved to be less eventful than the first. George rode on through the forest until he emerged at the rim of a deep canyon. It was a wide as a valley, George thought and very beautiful. He had never seen such colors that flowed in layers along the canyon walls. Peering carefully over the edge, he could see a river far below. It looked to be moving very swiftly.

Across the canyon in the distance were the Black Mountains. There was no way to cross here so George turned south and followed the rim for several miles. It was well past midday when he stopped at a small spring that bubbled out of a mossy rock. Nesset took a long drink and so did George. He also filled his water pouch and ate some figs. After a short rest in the shade, they continued.

The canyon widened, and the trail led down toward the river. George could see a crossing ahead. There were signs that others had crossed here too, foot prints of horses and wild animals on the bank. The sun was moving toward the western horizon, and George wanted to cross the river before dark. He nudged Nesset into the water. The river was shallow with a sandy bottom. Upon reaching the far side, he noticed the remains of many campfire and beyond them an elder wood.

George's eye caught a gleam that seemed to come from a tree at the edge of the wood. It sparkled off and on like a star. Humm, thought George, I will have to investigate that in the morning. He tied Nesset to the limb of a dead tree on the bank so he could drink and munch on grass. Then he gathered driftwood and, using his tinderbox, built a small fire. As he sat on a log gazing into it, he felt sad, lonely and homesick. This is not much fun, he grumbled to himself. He was sore and tired, and his sack of food was nearly empty.

He imagined being home in the castle. He could hear his mother singing as she drew back the heavy drapes and opened the shutters to let in the morning sun. He remembered a song that she often sang. It was about a young girl, the daughter of a shoemaker, who wanted to go to the ball, but had no fancy dress to wear and no way to buy one. But the girl dreamed of it anyway. She imagined the dress in every detail, sky blue with ribbons and lace. With her eyes closed, she saw herself wearing this dress. At night she dreamed of how it would feel as she stepped into the ballroom with the other beautiful ladies, and how a handsome young man would invite her to dance.

Then one day her father returned from delivering shoes to a nearby village and to her surprise he brought a bolt of blue satin and a basket of ribbons for her. Delighted and grateful, the young girl got to work sewing her gown with all the details that she had imagined.

Dance, dance, dance, across the ballroom floor.
Dream, dream your heart's desire, and life will give you more.

George repeated the last lines of the song again and again. Gradually, he began to realize that he had dreamed of being a knight, of wearing a suit of shiny armor, and of going on a grand adventure. And here he was. Life had given him his heart's desire. He felt better then, happy even. George rolled out his blanket on the grass and, and using a log as a pillow, he slept.

George dreamed. He was walking among the trees near where his body lay sleeping. He moved toward the flickering light hanging from a branch. It moved slightly and rainbows fell from it in waves. Beyond it he saw more lights, hundreds of them hanging in the trees by invisible threads. From them flowed a river of rainbows. He heard a tinkling as if the tiny lights were singing to each other. It was a pleasing sound, and it drew George deeper into the wood.

He felt like he was floating in the stream of color and soothing sounds. He was at peace. He thought he never wanted to leave this place. George felt as if he had become the light itself. He looked down at his dream body. It was shining, brilliant! He glimpsed tiny figures flitting around him, smiling, dancing.

And then he felt something else, a hard bumping against the side of his head, moist breath against his face, and he was hot! He woke with a start. Nesset whinnied in his ear.

Chapter 5

Allies

The sun was well up, and he was sweating inside his armor. He got up slowly using his saddle for support, then squatted by the river and splashed cold water on his face. He looked across at the old campfires left by others who had stopped here for the night. He wondered if they too had dreamed of the lights, and if they ever came out of the Tinkling Wood. If not, he thought, maybe they didn't have an ally like Nesset.

George shivered and stroked his horse's muzzle. "Thank you," he whispered. Glancing over to the tree where the glimmering light had been, he saw that it was gone and felt a bit sad.

The young knight ate the last biscuit and chunk of cheese before mounting. Kicking Nesset into a trot, they entered the wood. Emerging on the other side, he thought he heard a tinkle and a sigh.

The trail led up and out of the canyon onto an open plain. The grass was green and tall, rippled by a soft breeze. Upon reaching the far side, George and Nesset were confronted with a strange sight, two giant stones with the image of dragons carved into them. George stopped to look more closely. The dragons were just alike and faced each other as if protecting the trail between them. They were fierce and rather frightening.

Walking softly, Nesset moved between the stones and down a short track into a village. They passed a deserted smithy and a large empty corral. Several small huts with thatched roofs circled a well. Nothing stirred, and the only sound George heard was that of a goat bleating from behind one of the huts. He stopped at the well, pulled up a bucket of water and took a long drink. Then he emptied the bucket into a wooden trough beside the well for his horse.

George thought, how strange this was, a village with no people. The water was good, the site excellent, why was no one living here? At the far side of the circle was a stand of trees and some crude benches. George led Nesset into the shade and sat down. He was feeling very hungry and wondered when he would eat again. Closing his eyes, he thought of the excellent meals Cook made of partridge, rich brown gravy, bread with creamy butter, vegetables from her garden patch and pudding!

His mouth began to water when he felt eyes upon him. He was startled to see two small figures. One was a girl of about 10 and the other a boy maybe 6, probably her brother. Their hair was so blonde that it shone white. The girl carried a clay bowl, and George could smell soup. His stomach growled loudly. She silently offered the bowl to him along with a wooden spoon. The little boy set a cup of milk next to him on the bench. They stood back and watched him devour the food.

When he had finished, he handed the bowl and cup back to the girl with a nod and said, "Thank you." She nodded back unsmiling and began to turn away.

George called to her to wait. He stood and pulled out a pouch from under the saddle. Taking out a coin, he handed it to her. She stared at the coin as if she had never seen one before. He asked, "Are you the only people living in this village?"

She did not answer and he wondered if they spoke the same language. "Where are your parents?"

She looked at the ground and said "Fever, died." Just then, more children shuffled out of the huts and came to huddle behind the girl. All had the same white blonde hair. George counted eight. They were dirty and thin. George realized that sharing their food with him must have been a sacrifice.

He knew he could not leave them there. Besides the fact that, as a knight he was sworn to help those in need, his heart would not allow him to abandon these poor children. But he could not take them with him either. What could he do? He thought for a moment, and then had an idea.

He went to his pack and took out three pieces of parchment, a quill and the inkpot. He set to work drawing a map of the trail back to the castle. He marked the springs and safe places to rest, and put a big X on the tinkling wood so the little band would know what dangers to watch out for. Then he wrote a letter to Screemac asking that he grant them safe travel through the Stynix Wood. Lastly, he wrote a letter of introduction to his father.

He rolled up the two letters and, cutting hairs from Nesset's long tail, wrapped and tied them. After handing them to the girl, George said loudly so all the children could hear, "This is a map to my castle. It follows the trail on which I have come. Stay on the trail and heed my warnings." He pointed to the X on the map. "In the dark wood on the other side of the canyon live a clan of gnomes called the Stynix. If you see one, hand him this. They will give you safe passage.

When you reach the castle, tell the guard at the gate that you have a letter for Lord Aarrun from his son. You will be welcomed. On foot, the journey should take no more than five days. Take all the food you have and a blanket apiece. And may luck be with you until I see you again." And then thought, if I see you again.

George handed the map to the girl. She clutched it tightly to her chest and turned to look at her empty village. After a moment, she said, "We go." Without another word they went to their huts and came out with sacks and an old coat or blanket. She and her little brother joined the ragged band leading the goat. She nodded again to George and then set off down the track glancing up briefly at the dragon sentinels.

George called out to her, "Wait, why are there dragons at the entrance to this place? I must know."

The girl turned and said, in a voice George could barely hear, "They were our protectors long ago. They left before I was born."

Protectors, thought George quizzically, these dragons were their allies? He had never heard of such a thing. Looking after them, he murmured, "May you now be protected by all that is good in this world and find your way safely to Aarrun Castle."

George was aware of the haunted silence they left in their wake. Nothing stirred, not even a breeze. He shivered and knew that he did not want to spend the night in that deserted place. He led Nesset into the open, mounted and found the trail leading out of the village toward forbidding the mountains.

Chapter 6
The Storm

The trail wound between boulders and then began to climb. They had reached the hills that fronted the black mountains. The hills were covered with low growing, bright green plants that produced pink and purple flowers. The petals leaned to drink in the late afternoon sun, and wafted a sweet smell that reminded George of the rose garden his mother loved so much. He smiled at the memory. "I will tell her all about them when I get home. Yes, when I return!" he said to himself firmly.

His attention turned to the mountains that rose like a black wall before him, and to his quest. He remembered the stories of the dragon he had heard so many times when he was young. He envisioned it as gigantic, black and vicious, with fierce red eyes and razor sharp teeth. Its shadow darkened the valley and struck fear in all who lived there.

What was I thinking? He asked himself as he rode toward his fate. Yes, he had been trained well by his father's master of the guard. And yes, he had won tournaments against the other young knights who had come to the castle to challenge him. But somehow, jousting with a knight of seventeen seemed to pale against the might of a fire breathing dragon.

George shook his head and said out loud, "My friend, what have I gotten us into?" Nesset lifted his head and flicked his ears backward. "What am I trying to prove, eh?"

As if to answer, his father's voice echoed in the young knight's head. They had been sitting in the garden late one evening talking about the journey to come. His father had said, "George, you have all that is needed to be a champion. You are strong and well trained in all manner of warrior arts. You ride well and have an excellent horse to carry you. However, many knights possess these. What you have that lifts you above them all is a keen intelligence. You gather information quickly and do not come hasty conclusions, and you have a big heart. All of these qualities make you wise beyond your years. And you are clever! That will be a great asset as you face the challenges ahead. Do not doubt yourself, my son. You will succeed where others have not."

Although these words were said many months ago, George heard them as if his father was riding beside him and felt comforted. He even looked over to see if his father was there, but saw only the low hills.

And as he looked at those hills, he realized they had turned from bright green to gray and the flowers had folded up. His gaze went to the sky where heavy dark clouds had gathered. Lightning flashed followed by a massive crash of thunder.

George kicked Nesset into a gallop and headed for an outcrop of rocks ahead. The wind began to blow cold and angry, howling down from the mountains. George dismounted and led Nesset through a jumble of stones to a shallow cave that he had seen from the trail. It was on a ledge which Nesset had to lunge to reach.

There was just room enough for the two of them under the overhanging stone. They watched the lightning illuminate the land and listened to the thunder roar and roll. George thought, it sounds like monsters battling in the sky. Then the rain came, sheeting off the ledge above them, completely hiding the view below.

George felt very grateful for the shelter. He took Nesset's leather food bag off the saddle, thrust it into the rain until it was filled and held it for Nesset to drink. Then he too drank from his leather pouch and sat down with his back to the wall. He was tired and hungry. It had been a long day. He dozed on and off throughout the night. When he woke, it was still raining and totally dark. It is as black as a witch's kettle. He smiled at the thought. That was Cook's favorite saying.

Except, what was this? His eye caught a faint glimmer which seemed to be coming from the pile of stones near his feet. He reached toward it, aware that he could not even see his hand in the blackness. Moving the stones away, he uncovered an orb. It was the size of his palm and gave off a hazy red glow.

He picked it up and peered at it intently. Gradually, the menacing eye of a dragon took shape. It was fiery red and looked directly at George. He gasped and dropped the orb. Then he scrunched back against the wall of the cave, not wanting to touch it again. The orb lay glowing softly.

George was trembling with fear. He took out his rabbit's foot and held it tightly to calm himself. He was aware of how alone and vulnerable he was. He wondered if the dragon could see him with that eye and knew that he was there. Maybe it had sent the storm to stop or even destroy him! Eventually, exhaustion overcame the young knight, and he slept again.

George woke to bird song and Nesset's soft whinny. He stood slowly and looked down at the orb which was still at his feet. Now it reflected only a milky white and did not seem dangerous at all. George picked it up and held it in his hand. Maybe he dreamed the eye of the dragon. After all, he had been thinking about the beast all day. He did not know, but he decided to take the orb with him, so he put it in his pack.

Leading Nesset down the slippery slope back to the trail, George was aware of the smell of fresh sage. The world had been washed clean. As he mounted, George's only worry was the gnawing hunger in his belly.

Chapter 7

The Offering

George rode upward. The hills were becoming steeper and the trail narrower. The hillsides were mostly a jumble of rock. A few stubby trees grew in the cracks here and there. At last he came to a grassy glade with a small stream running through it. He dismounted and let his horse graze. At least Nesset won't be hungry, he thought.

Kneeling by the stream, George caught his refection in the water. Besides the fact that his face was dirty, it looked changed. Who was that staring back? He felt unsettled, but he was too tired and hungry to think about it. He plunged his hands into the cold stream and washed his face, which helped a little.

The light glinting off the water reminded him of the orb. He got it out of his pack and sat down on a rock. The orb had not changed since the morning. It still swirled with a white milky light. He shrugged and set it on the rock while he filled his water pouch. The orb glowed red for just a moment and then went white again. George did not notice.

It was nearly midday when George and Nesset left the pleasant spot and headed up the trail. The land seemed to be getting wilder, and he was surrounded by huge jagged stones. At one point, George had to dismount so that Nesset could squeeze between two boulders. It felt good to walk, so he continued on foot, but after a while, he began to feel weak from hunger and mounted again.

The temperature was dropping even though the sun was still high. He reached around and untied his helmet and bedroll from behind him on the saddle. He put on the helmet and wrapped the thick woolen blanket around his shoulders. He sent a grateful thank you to the weaver, a kind old woman of the village whose back was bent from years of working her loom. The blanket was warm and George thought, I may starve, but at least I won't freeze.

He felt the gnawing in his stomach. "Ahhh," he moaned, "this is unbearable." Then he got hold of his thoughts. No, I will think of something else. He began creating the story of his return home in triumph. At first the farmers would see him and wave as they came running to the road. The fishermen would leave their nets to join them. He saw himself crossing the drawbridge and heard the guards yell, "He's back!!! Sir George has returned!" By the time he reached the court yard, it would be full of town folk, and the people from the land would pour in behind him.

In his imagination, he heard them shouting and laughing, "He's back, our hero, dragon slayer has returned!" He would ride to the steps of the great hall. His mother and father would rush out and smile in happy amazement.

Oh, George thought, it will be a grand homecoming. I will have many stories to tell, and there will be a great feast! He imagined the long tables in the great hall covered with mounds of food. He could smell the cooked squash, the fresh bread and roast mutton. He closed his eyes as he enjoyed his imagined glory, allowing his horse to plod up the trail.

George had a smile on his face. He thought he could even smell the roast mutton. Then he lifted his head and sniffed. He could smell roast mutton!

Nesset had stopped beside a large flat rock next to the trail. George looked down and saw a golden platter with a big chunk of meat on it, nicely browned. Next to it was a flagon and a golden goblet.

George threw off his blanket, and leaped to the ground. He took a big bite of the mutton. It had been cooked to perfection with tasty herbs and oils, but George did not notice this due to his desperate hunger. He tore into it and chewed with delight. Then poured some light golden mead into the goblet and drank.

He stopped and looked around. This was not right, he realized with a sinking feeling. What was a delicious plate of food doing here in this wild place? On all sides, the dark rocks hemmed the trail. It was totally quiet, not a sign of life. George looked at the mutton in one hand and the goblet in his other. This was not a mirage. He could taste it and feel the hunger pangs in his stomach receding. More slowly and cautiously, George continued eating while keeping his eyes on the trail.

Nothing happened for several minutes. Then George heard a queer sound. It was music and it seemed to be coming from the golden platter. George moved away and stared at it. He was not so eager to investigate after his experience with the orb the night before. But his curiosity got the best of him. He set the food down on the rock and held up the platter. As George peered at it, words in red letters flowed across it. They said, Welcome, Sir Knight, I have been waiting for you. Yours truly, Scraggin.

George dropped the platter, the crash jarring the silence. The DRAGON! It had to be, waiting for me! He knows I am coming. He left this food to lure me into a trap, and here I am. I walked right into it!

He pulled his sword and shield off the saddle and stood on the trail. He was shaking and sweating and afraid. But he stood anyway. This is it, George thought, this is what I came for. He practiced swinging his sword and discovered that his body was quite sore and was not moving well at all. That made him even more frightened. His teeth began to chatter, which sounded like a hammer in his helmet.

No dragon came, all was still. George was tiring. His fear had worn him out. Not to mention the fact that he had slept badly the night before and had been riding for days. Finally, he let his sword down and took a big breath. His heart had stopped pounding. Now he felt confused. What should he do?

He went back to the rock, drank some more mead and rested. So, he thought more calmly, the meeting is not to happen here on the trail. Well, there is nothing for it, I must go to him. He tied his bedroll back on his saddle and mounted Nesset, who had been watching George curiously throughout this episode. Resigned to his fate, the young knight urged his horse to continue up the mountain.

Chapter 8

Scraggin

Tense and on guard, George steeled himself for the coming battle. He reviewed the moves he had learned in knight's training, and he recalled how the sword master had praised him for his natural skill and balance. This study was interrupted by another thought, Yours truly? The message had signed off with yours truly. Would a dragon say that? He wondered in amazement. And Scraggin, what kind of a name is that for a dragon? Maybe it wasn't his foe after all. Maybe it was an ally, a kindly old man who knew a few magic tricks. Maybe he too was the dragon's enemy and wanted George's help to destroy it.

These ideas made George feel some better and he relaxed a bit. It was late evening, and he realized he would need to find a place to stop for the night. He knew he would not sleep, but he did not want Nesset stumbling on the trail in the dark. A narrow path led to the left between two boulders. George reined on to it. He hoped to find a sheltered spot and maybe some twigs with which to build a small fire. Contemplating how a fire would warm and cheer him, he was surprised when Nesset came to an abrupt stop. Then George saw it, standing before him was, well ...... something.

"Hello!" said the strange green creature jubilantly. It was dressed in a rust colored cloak over a long black robe. Big green claw like feet stuck out from under it. The creature appeared to be a head taller than George. It leaned on a staff topped with an orb much like the one George had found in the cave. It had short white horns, a long blackened snout and bright black eyes. Not red, George noted. It was smiling, or at least George thought that was a smile. It did have many very sharp teeth.

"Welcome, welcome, my good knight. I am Scraggin, and I am so pleased you have come." Scraggin turned and sort of waddled toward the recess of a cave. George then saw his tail, a long curved green thing sticking out from under the back of its robe. Scraggin stopped and waved to George to follow.

George was totally confused. He just sat in his saddle and stared. This was a dragon? This is what I have come to fight? This is the fierce monster the stories were told about, the very dragon that had killed all the brave knights that came before? George's mind boggled. He could not move. Nesset stood very still, ears pointed toward the strange creature.

Scraggin waddled back and stood before them. "Well, are you going to come in out of the cold and dark or not?" He sounded a bit impatient. "It can be dangerous out here at night." he warned.

George stuttered, "Ah ummm, you are a dragon, I take it?"

"Of course I'm a dragon!" Scraggin replied rather annoyed. "What do I look like, a turtle? Turtles don't have horns." At that Scraggin giggled, an odd chortling sound George had never heard before, and would never forget.

"Come on then," he said, "I have just made my fabulous mutton and dumpling stew with plum pudding for desert. You do like plum pudding, don't you?"

George's stomach growled loudly. His body dismounted in spite of his confusion. He loved plum pudding. He led

Nesset into the mouth of large cave. There was a pile of hay and a bucket of water sitting next to the wall. Nesset began to munch on the hay. In a daze, George walked deeper into the cave, keeping his sword and shield with him. Scraggin was holding open a heavy tapestry door.

They entered a large room with a thick carpet of red, green and gold. It was more lush and beautiful than any at the castle. On one side was a fireplace with a smoke hole that opened into the rock above it, over the fire hung a black kettle. George could smell the savory stew. To the left of the fireplace was a bench cut into the stone wall. It was covered with what looked like a red velvet cushion. To the right was a cupboard in which golden plates, bowls, cups, and goblets were displayed. Several oversized pillows were strewn about the floor. George noticed another opening toward the back of the cave, but it was too dark to see into.

Scraggin was watching George. "Well," he asked, "what do you think of my lair, eh? Quite comfy, wouldn't you say?"

George could not find his voice, "Ah um um." he mumbled still looking around the room. His eyes rested on a large book laid on a stone table. It appeared to be bound in leather and had strange raised markings on the cover.

Scraggin said conversationally, "That is my journal. I write in it all that I have learned and even what I think about. It is my guide and my friend."

"Now," he said rubbing his clawed hands together, "let's eat!"

He took two bowls from the cupboard and filled each with a good helping of stew. Then he drew out two large soup spoons from a round golden vase. He motioned George to the bench and said heartily, "Sit, dig in." and he handed him a bowl.

Scraggin dug in. He slurped rather noisily and drained the last from the bowl. George was still holding his bowl and spoon. Scraggin looked indignant, "I thought you were hungry! What was all that moaning about? EAT!"

This shook George out of his stupor. He took off his helmet and set it and his weapons on the bench. Then he ate. The stew was delicious, the best he had ever tasted, even better than Cook's. But of course, I was starving, he thought.

Scraggin smiled his toothy grin and dished up two bowls of pudding. He ate his pudding a little slower and with relish. George also enjoyed every bite.

When they both had finished, Scraggin set the bowls on the hearth and said, "I will wash up later. You are probably in need of rest, as you didn't get much last night. I am a bit pooped myself. This has been a very exciting day! Eh? Pull up a pillow and make yourself at home." To which the dragon gathered up some pillows, lay down on the luxurious carpet and went right to sleep.

George did feel exhausted. It seemed like his armor weighed more than a millstone. He pulled open the tapestry door and spoke to Nesset. "Are you all right?" He whispered. He went over to stroke his horse's neck. Nesset whinnied softly. "I don't know what to make of this, so be ready to leave in the night. I will stay alert." George felt comforted by Nesset's presence.

He went back in and lay down with a pillow under his head. Scraggin was snoring. This was not what I expected. He stared at the odd creature. This is not what I expected at all. George didn't want to sleep, but his body thought otherwise. He yawned and closed his eyes.

Chapter 9

The Myth

George woke to an empty cave. He bolted up right and wished he hadn't. Every part of him ached. A fire was burning merrily on the hearth, and an iron teakettle was steaming over it. Scraggin entered from the door at the back. He said cheerily, "Good morning brave knight!"

George glared. It did not seem so good to him. Scraggin took down two cups and began making tea. George realized that he was teetering a bit. He shuffled over to the stone bench and sat down.

"Here you go." Scraggin said while handing him a cup. "That will fix you right up."

George's cup paused in the air. "What is it?" he asked suspiciously.

"Tea!" Scraggin said, "Made from rosehips and motherwort, it's good for calming the nerves." He smiled and George could see all his teeth. Somehow he was not reassured, but he drank anyway. It tasted fruity, a bit sweet and very good.

Scraggin invited, "Why don't you take off that armor and be comfortable. You are safe here."

George shook his head. "NO!" he said rather forcefully. "If it's all the same to you." he added more softly.

Scraggin shrugged, "Suit yourself." Then he giggled at his pun. "Suit yourself....get it?" and laughed again.

The tea seemed to relieve George's muscles and he relaxed a bit. "Scraggin," he demanded, "are you the dragon that has been terrorizing the people around here? Burning their huts and stealing their livestock, and, and, and" he sputtered, "eating young maidens?"

"Oh that." Scraggin replied. "There was a time, many eons ago, mind you, that my kind did a bit of harassing of the locals, which has given dragons a nasty reputation. And there is still a bit of truth to the rumors even today."

George grabbed his sword and stood facing Scraggin. The dragon frowned and waved a claw at him. "Now, now, don't get all worked up. A dragon's got to eat doesn't he? I do a little magic to maintain the illusion, and while the villages are hiding, I nab a sheep or two and, occasionally, a goat. I prefer mutton. Goat tends to be stringy, makes a good stew though. I like to use thyme and wild sage with goat. I will show you my herb garden later on. It's out back."

As Scraggin rattled on, George held his stance, but slowly he let his sword drop. Then he pointed it at Scraggin again and asked accusingly, "What about all those knights who never returned?"

"Well, now there's a story in that." The dragon nodded sagely while refilling George's cup, "You noticed the remains of camp fires near the river? Didn't you wonder if those who built them made it past the Tinkling Wood, and what about the Stynix? Not all knights are as noble and willing to help as you were. The Stynix are not as harmless and they look. And those storms! They have bested many a traveler, believe me."

George narrowed his eyes, "So you did send the storm to stop me?"

"No, no." answered Scraggin, "These Mountains have been making their own weather since before there were dragons. I do not interfere."

"You're telling me that you had nothing to do with the disappearances?"

"Nothing." said Scraggin shaking his head. "But I do not discourage the grisly tales either."

"Why?" asked George, now totally baffled. He had let his sword down again.

"Well," said Scraggin, "you know how it is when you have important work to do, and young lads who want to prove themselves come hammering at your cave every other month? I need peace and quiet!"

With this, George sat down on the bench with a heavy thud. He thought for a moment and then looked up, "So what am I doing here?"

"Ah," exclaimed Scraggin, "now we are getting to the mutton of the matter! I am so glad you asked….finally." He finished with a disgusted grunt. George frowned. He was totally confused.

Scraggin said airily, "All will be made clear, not to worry. But for now, you should tend to your horse, yes?"

"Nesset!" George thought with a start. He went out the tapestry door. Nesset whinnied to him as he approached. A fresh pile of hay and a full bucket of water had been provided. George rubbed his muzzle. "How are you my friend?" Then he pulled down his pack and dragged off the saddle, leaning it against the cave wall. "There," he said rubbing the horse's broad back "looks like we are safe enough, for now at least." He pressed his forehead against Nesset's side. None of this made much sense, but he didn't feel threatened, just hungry again. Why did Scraggin want him here? There must be a reason behind it. And what work was he speaking of? He signed, "We'll find out soon enough I expect." He gave him a pat and moved to the door thinking about breakfast.

Chapter 10

The Wizard

When George entered, Scraggin was busy at the hearth, humming to himself. He wore a purple cloak with vines and leaves woven on it. He stirred a pot over the fire, then took a spoon from the vase and tasted his creation. "Hummm, needs a bit more cinnamon." He murmured, and put in a pinch from a jar on the hearth.

George shook his head, a dragon that liked to cook. No one back at the castle would believe him.

Scraggin turned and saw George. "There you are! Would you like some porridge? My special recipe," he said with a wink. And that was a strange sight indeed!

George took the initiative and brought two bowls over to the pot. Scraggin ladled in the porridge and then exclaimed, "Oh, oh, don't forget the berries!" He lifted a bowl of ripe thimble berries from the hearth and poured some into each bowl. "There now," he sighed, "doesn't that make a pretty breakfast?"

George shook his head again in amazement and took his bowl to the bench. He had claimed it as his spot. Scraggin clearly was not made to sit on anything but the floor.

George had never been partial to porridge, but this was quite good. He ate it all and set the bowl on the bench. "There is something else I want to know," he said with more curiosity that suspicion. "How do you know about my journey here?"

Scraggin smiled, "You are a smart one after all." He stood back a little and announced with a deep voice, "Sir George, Knight of the Realm, I am Scraggin, 84th Illustrious Wizard Dragon of the Air Clan. I am only 410 of your years old, which is quite young for a dragon. Does that answer your question?"

"Not really." said George cocking his head to one side. "So you are a wizard, and you can see in far off places? You were watching me?" he asked.

"Well not exactly, scrying is a skill I possess, but don't use very often. It's just that there have been many who have traveled the road before you did, besides knights you understand, and they carried tales of their own to me. And all right," he admitted, "I do have magical means of knowing what others are doing, but do you really think I would share those secrets with you? We've just met for newt's sake!"

Before George could reply to this, Scraggin declared, "Well, now that we've been properly introduced, come, I have much to show you." And with that he waddled toward the door in the back of the cave.

George followed rather stiffly. He was thinking it would be such a relief to take off his armor. He had to duck a bit to walk through the low door into the next room. Burning brightly were several large candles set on tall pedestals around the room. This floor was not carpeted but smooth dark stone. The clicking of his boots sounded odd in the silence.

Scraggin didn't seem to notice. He was now all business. "Come, come." he said a bit impatiently.

George walked slowly across the floor, eyes widening as he went. On either side of him were shelves loaded with jars, baskets, and scrolls. What was in them? George wasn't sure he wanted to know. At the back was a long table with all sorts of strange objects on it, and above that was a round window.

Scraggin had pulled open the shutters and exclaimed, "Fresh air!" Then he turned to George who had stopped in the middle of the room. "What is it?" demanded the dragon.

George was staring at a creature perched on a pole. It was black and looked rather like a large bat but had a bigger body and a dragon shaped head. It was hissing and spitting little streams of flame at him. Scraggin laughed, "That's just Harpy. She's my familiar. Every wizard must have a familiar, you know, and Harpy is quite talented. She is a shape shifter which comes in very handy, and she is a scandalous gossip."

"Come." he said again and crossed the room to another door. He paused before the little dragon and they touched noses. "My little Harpy, I bet you would like a snack." With that, he reached under the lid of a large basket setting on the floor and pulled out a small live mouse by the tail. Harpy snatched it out of his fingers and swallowed it in one gulp. Scraggin beamed at her and waddled on. George hugged the wall as he passed the tiny fire breathing dragon. She shot a flame that nearly singed his hair.

The next room was lit from a larger window above a rough wooden table, and beyond that was another opening. This room smelled strongly of herbs and was very clean. George also noticed several cloaks hanging from pegs in one corner.

Scraggin said, "This is my workshop." It too had shelves along one wall with baskets full of dried plants. Bundles of herbs were hanging beneath the table. They smelled of sage and lavender.

Scraggin had already moved out the door so George followed him into a large garden. It was the most unusual garden

George had ever seen. Many of the plants he recognized from the gardens at home, herbs like fennel, thyme, and mint. Farther along were vegetables, beans growing on tall poles, squash and carrots. There were also strange looking things that moved even though there was no wind. One dark purple plant snapped at him as he walked by. There were flowers too, geraniums and forget-me-nots. Some had brilliant blossoms as big as his hand. When he bent to smell one, Scraggin called out, "I wouldn't do that if I were you. They are called wilting palms, and they will wilt you for sure." he giggled. George pulled back quickly.

Scaggin continued through the garden and out an archway made of twigs. George followed and found himself on the ledge of a cliff. He peered over the edge and caught his breath. It must have been a thousand feet down to the mist below. George looked out over a swirling sea of white that seemed to go on forever. Above it the sky was crystalline blue, not a cloud disturbed the vastness. "Beautiful." he muttered.

"Yes," signed Scraggin blissfully, "this is my favorite spot." He had taken off his cloak and laid it on the ground. George watched with fascination as Scraggin unfolded his wings. They were only about 4 feet long, green with flecks of gold in the webbing between the bones. Scraggin stretched them to their full length, turned to face the cave, and began fanning them slowly in the warm air.

George ventured, "Can you fly with those?"

Scraggin said, "No, I can fly alright, but not with these. You see when I hatched, my wings were not fully developed as in other dragons of my kind. So I became a wizard." He said this in a very matter of fact way. "I must air them out every day or they get moldy, and that is no fun, I can assure you!"

Stranger and stranger, thought George. He reviewed what he had seen so far, a rather odd looking dragon with short wings, who likes to cook, and who lives in a cave with carpeting and velvet pillows. He doesn't appear to be threatening or even scary. In fact, he has been very friendly and helpful. But it all seemed too strange, and George was not convinced that there was nothing to fear from this creature. He was determined to stay alert and learn more before deciding what to do next.

Chapter 11

The Task

They were quiet for a while enjoying the sunny day and the view. Then Scraggin instructed in a more serious tone, "Sit, we must talk."

George sat on a handy boulder, his armor creaking. "I have a task for you. You did come here for an adventure, yes?" he asked briskly. George did not answer.

"Well first," said Scraggin, "let me tell you a little story. Before your kind came to this place, that was around 800 of your years ago, this was the home of many dragons. We lived on mountain tops and hunted the wild deer and boar that roamed the forest. It was a good life. I was hatched on top of this very mountain with my brother and sister.

When we were just young chicks, humans came to the valley. They cut down the forest, planted fields and built the castle. My kind did indeed have great sport with them, which is where all those gruesome stories came from. Also around that time, the earth shifted and the weather changed. It gradually became warmer, too warm for air dragons.

So my clan flew off in a great caravan to a range of higher mountains far away. Every dragon left, save for myself and my uncle. His name is Haftnor. He still lives in the cave on the peak above."

George could see a dark jagged peak beyond the top of the cave. He felt rather sorry for Scraggin at that moment. He was an orphan. George asked sympathetically, "Do you see your uncle often?"

"Ohhh no, he has grown bitter and angry and just a little crazy. He believes the humans are the reason for the climate change. He broods and plots ways to get rid of them. He has become a danger to your kind and, I believe, even to me."

George brightened up, "You want me to destroy this dragon?"

"No," Scraggin said patiently. "I want you to convince him to leave, to go and join our clan in that distant land."

"What?" George exclaimed, jumping up from his rock. "You want me to talk to a crazy dragon? He would toast me and eat me for dinner!"

"Yes," admitted Scraggin, "that is a possibility. But you will have an incentive to offer him. Something that will make him want to leave."

George stared at him incredulously, "And what would that be? No, don't answer that. Why aren't you the one to convince him? You are his nephew!"

Scraggin sighed, "But I have tried many times. He will not listen to me. Not only am I his small relative, but I am a wizard. He has little respect."

George huffed in disgust, marched into the cave and sat on his bench. After a while, Scraggin came in carrying a basket of dark material. On top was a large pair of spectacles. He put on the glasses and began stitching the cloth. The dragon's clawed fingers were remarkably agile, George noted in spite of his dark mood. He glared in suspicious silence.

Finally, Scraggin had finished and held up a cloak with a hood. It was as black as night. He nodded in satisfaction. "Yes, that should do." he said. "Here try it on."

Reluctantly George allowed him to drape the cloak around his shoulders and draw up the hood. He was completely covered, even his face was hidden. "Perfect!" exclaimed Scraggin.

"This is the incentive?" George asked sarcastically.

"No, my young knight, this is your camouflage. You see my uncle's eye sight has become rather dim in recent years. Wearing this, he will never see you. And he mumbles to himself, so he will not hear you either."

"Great," said George, "so I can get close enough for him to bite off my head. But how am I going to convince him to leave?"

"Yes well," Scraggin smiled, "we will discuss that later. Now let's go for a swim. You could really use one." And he crinkled up his nose. 'Come, I have packed a lunch!" He looked at George and frowned, "But you must take off that squeaky armor, and bring your pack. It's a bit of a walk to the lake." With that he picked up a basket from the hearth and strolled out the door.

George contemplated his situation for a few minutes and decided that Scraggin was not going to harm him, not directly anyway. So he unbuckled his armor and pulled the chain mail over his head. It was a relief to be free of it. He thought, whew! I do need a bath! Picking up his pack he followed the wizard outside. He patted Nesset as he walked by and assured him, "We'll be back soon." Nesset whinnied and continued munching hay. George thought that his horse seemed quite contented, and that he deserved a rest.

They walked to the main trail and up the mountain. After about half a mile, Scraggin turned to the right onto a narrow path. It lead between tall rocks and opened into a stand of evergreens. They followed it down to a small lake.

When they reached a pebbled beach, Scraggin dug in the basket and handed George a cake of pink soap that smelled like roses. "Here," he instructed, "use this." Then he set the basket down, took off his cloak and robe and waddled out into the water.

George was once again amazed as he watched Scraggin dog paddle around the lake. What next? He wondered. Then he too took off his dirty tunic and pants and pushed them into the water at the edge of the lake. Taking the soap, he slowly walked in up to his chest. He was not fond of swimming. He had been taught to swim in the river by the fishermen, but he still didn't feel comfortable in deep water.

The water was cold but George got used to it. He lathered up all over, rinsed, then came out and scrubbed his dirty cloths. After hanging them on some bushes, lay in the sun to dry off.

He could hear Scraggin singing loudly, "There once was a dragon named Tootles, who loved to make noodles, then one day she cooked up a mess, and they all turned to snakes and ate her. Ha ha ha!" he laughed. George wondered who was crazier, Scraggin or Haftnor.

Eventually the dragon waddled back to the beach and began unpacking the picnic basket. George had dressed the in clean clothes from his pack and was feeling more at ease and talkative. He asked, "Do other dragons like to swim?"

Scraggin shrugged, "I have no idea." he said, "I will say that I have never heard tell of it. But then again, I am an unusual dragon." He winked, which again made George stare.

George ventured, "Ummm, how is that?" thinking of all the strange things he had witnessed in the past two days.

"Since I was a chick," Scraggin began, "I have been interested in magic. Oh yes, we dragons possess powers that humans cannot imagine. But I wanted to know how the magic worked." He continued shaking his head, "And this not was very popular with my family."

"After years of questioning and experimenting, my parents decided to send me to apprentice with the dragon wizard who lived on the other side of these mountains. I could not fly there myself, of course, so I had to be carried. I was not as big as I am now. But still, it was humiliating. However, I was so excited at the prospect of having my questions answered that I went willingly."

Scraggin continued, "Shinoz is the 83rd Illustrious Wizard Dragon of our line. And he is a mighty wizard indeed. I lived with him for about 100 years until I had learned all that I could, and then returned home. Do you want to know the most important lesson I learned from Shinoz?" asked the dragon.

"Yes!" George said enthusiastically.

"Keep a clean cave, dirt piles up and gets in the way." Scraggin said matter of factly. "Shinoz was the fussiest dragon I have ever met."

George was confused, "What does that have to do with magic?"

"Not a lot, actually." replied Scraggin with a grin. "Don't look so disappointed. There is much for you to learn."

With that Scraggin handed George a hunk of cold mutton and a ripe pear. He took the pear and looked at it, "This is a pear, how did a pear come to be up here?"

"Ah," smiled the dragon mysteriously, "just a bit of my magic. Finish up now, we must be off home." He put on his robe and cloak, picked up the basket and headed up the trail.

George considered that after 100 years of studying magic, Scraggin would know quite a lot indeed, and he followed.

Chapter 12

The Student

George was full of questions. They seemed to bubble up inside of him so fast he could barely catch them before they floated away. He tried to focus his thoughts. He wanted to know more about magic and how to use it, but clearly Scraggin was not going to share his secrets just yet.

By this time, they had reached the turn off to the dragon's cave. All thoughts of magic flew out of his head when George saw a strange creature standing next to Nesset. It was about four feet tall and covered in course black hair. It turned toward them as they approached. Its head was round with huge eyes, tall pointy ears and a lopsided mouth that showed a few large square teeth. It was rather ugly.

George shouted, "Hey, get away from my horse!" The odd creature scurried over the rocks.

Scraggin laid a clawed hand on George's arm. "It's only my ogre," he said, "not to worry."

George hurried over to Nesset. He stroked his neck and murmured, "Are you well my friend?" Nessett gave him a low whiney and rubbed his head against George's chest. George saw that fresh hay and water had appeared. He looked questioningly at Scraggin. "What is an ogre?"

Scraggin waved him to follow, "Come in and I will explain."

A fire was burning in the fireplace and logs were piled high against the wall. These had not been there when they left, George knew.

"This ogre is very small for his kind, a runt if you will." Scraggin began. "He came to me many years ago with a large gash in his head. He had been hacked by a human who had caught him in the henhouse. I bandaged and cared for him until he recovered, and he has been here ever since. He lives in a hollow tree and comes every day to tend to my basic needs. He is shy, enormously helpful, and a wonderful herder of sheep, if you get my meaning." There was that wink again. George wished he wouldn't do that.

"Let's have a cup of tea." Scraggin brought out the tea cups and poured the hot water from the kettle into them. Then he put in a pinch of black leaves. "That should set for a few minutes." He said. "In the meantime, let us speak about your task."

Scraggin sat on a pillow and wiggled until he was comfortable. "Ahhh," he signed, "that's nice. Anyway," he went on, "my uncle is a craggy old snag for sure, but he has a soft spot. He has always wanted to have a family of his own, but for some reason or another, probably due to his nasty personality, he has not been successful in attracting a mate."

With this, Scraggin launched into a tale that was as strange as George had ever heard. "But I know of a dragon's egg that still lays here in these mountains. It was stolen by a griffin who calls herself Drugina. Seems to me she has illusions of grandeur, thinking she is some kind of dragon." He said huffily. "Anyway, she has been sitting on that egg for eons hoping it will hatch, no doubt. But this is not possible. For a dragon to come out of its shell, both a mother and father have to sing it out when it is time. Without this, the dragon will not emerge."

George asked, "The baby dragon still lives?"

"Oh yes, dragons are eternal unless they are killed outright." This was news to George, but then again, he thought, just about everything he had experienced here was unheard of until now.

"What does this egg have to do with getting Haftnor to join the other dragons?" he wondered.

"That's where you come in. I am charging you, Sir Knight, with the task of stealing the egg back and sneaking it into my uncle's lair. As crazy as he is, he knows he cannot hatch or raise a dragon chick on his own. It takes a clan, you know." He smiled at that. "Haftnor will feel duty bound to take it to the distant land. In fact, he will be happy to do so. The new addition will be his responsibility. Isn't that a fabulous plan? Am I not a genius?" Scraggin beamed.

George had not gotten his head around this enough to respond. When he did, he jumped up and shouted loudly, "And just how am I supposed to STEAL an egg from an insane griffin?" He was breathing heavily now, his eyes darting around the room as if looking for an escape.

"Oh dear," Scraggin said in a rather disappointed voice, "I guess I didn't do that very well. Never mind. Here, sit down and drink your tea."

George's heart beat returned to normal as he sat sipping from the cup Scraggin had handed him. He heard of griffins all right, but had never seen one. They were said to be giant creatures, half bird with a large wicked beak and wings, and half lion with a long tail. Their front feet had talons and their back carried sharp claws. And they preyed on humans!

Well, he thought to himself. I did come here to do something important for my people. It sounds like this Haftnor is the real threat. How hard could it be to steal an egg anyway? George took a deep breath and let it out slowly. "Ok," he said reluctantly, "What am I supposed to do?"

Scraggin put on his glasses and waddled over to the big book on the stone table. He motioned for George to follow.

The young knight joined him and watched Scraggin as he held the book on its binding and let it fall open. He then instructed. "Close your eyes, take your finger and just put it anywhere on the page."

"Is this some kind of magic?" asked George.

"Yes," Scraggin replied, "it is a form of magic."

George did as he was told and then opened his eyes. He read, "Warning, do not eat moldy sassafras, it will give you scale blight."

George frowned at Scraggin, who giggled. "Magic isn't always precise. Let's see," he read the passage just above. "Griffins are fierce and unfriendly creatures, but they do have a weakness. They cannot resist mead. After drinking only a flagon or so, they will fall into a deep sleep that lasts for several hours. Ah ha!" Scraggin cried startling George, "That is your answer!"

"Mead." George said flatly.

"Mead!" Scraggin cried again jubilantly. He looked at George's face which had taken one shock too many. "Humm," I think you have had enough for one day. Why don't you sit down and I will make us a nice salad before we sleep. Tomorrow we will work on our plan."

George eased himself down on the pillows in a daze and murmured, "Mead."

Scraggin waddled out the back door to the garden and returned a few minutes later with a bowl of fresh vegetables. George was nearly asleep, but he heard the dragon say thoughtfully, "He'll do, he'll do."

Chapter 13

The Plan

George woke to a horrible smell. He looked over toward the fire and spied the teakettle and a pot of porridge, but he knew the smell did not come from those. He made his way through the door to the laboratory where Scraggin was standing behind the table talking to himself. As George approached, he saw jars filled with odd things, animal parts, dead spiders, strange looking roots. There was a cauldron filled with glowing coals, and a flask with a dark bubbling liquid suspended above it. In the center was a large bowl into which Scraggin was adding bits of this and that. The odor was unspeakable. George exclaimed, "Ugggg!"

Scraggin looked up and smiled, "It is rather nasty, I admit, but that is necessary for the job it is to do."

George held his nose and asked, "And what would that be. Or do I really want to know?"

Scraggin said airily, "Away with you, I am nearly finished."

George returned to the outer chamber and made two cups of tea. Scraggin entered looking very satisfied. He carried a scroll. "The salve will need to set for a few hours."

George crinkled up his nose and said, "So we have to live with that smell all day?"

Scraggin nodded, "You, my brave knight, will be smelling it a lot longer than that. By rubbing it on your armor, your human smell will be masked, and Drugina will not get a whiff of you. She will think you are just some old meat she has in storage for a hungry day."

George rolled his eyes. This is not getting any better, he thought.

"Now," continued Scraggin, as he unrolled the parchment. "This is a map of the mountain where the griffin lives. It is about a day's journey from here as the dragon flies, but the land is rough so it will take you longer." Using a long claw, Scraggin pointed out the trail that led from his mountain retreat to the griffin's nest. "The last part will be the hardest as you will have to do some climbing."

George glared. He had never climbed anything except onto the back of his horse.

At that moment, George noticed the orb on Scraggin's staff, which was standing by the front door, begin to glow red. Scraggin followed his gaze and went to retrieve it. "Ah!" he said triumphantly, "The ogre has scrounged up some mead." He stared into the orb for a full minute, and then it went white.

George, remembering the orb he had found during the storm, asked cautiously, "Is that how you watch others?"

"No, but it is a method of communication. By focusing intently into the orb, you can send messages. The ogre just sent an image of a large cask of mead. We are in luck!" Scraggin seemed very pleased. George did not share the feeling.

Scraggin turned back to the map. "You should reach to the Beech Wood by night fall. It is a large stand of trees just off the trail. You can't miss it." He pointed to a circle of trees. "Rise early so you can pass the swamp before noon. The trail follows the edge of the swamp here." Scraggin pointed again. "Swamp rats are very dangerous. They especially like horse flesh." George pulled back in alarm.

"Not to worry, they are also mesmerized by shiny things." Scraggin pulled a bag from his cloak. He opened it and showed George a large crystal.

George held it and remarked, "It is beautiful."

"Isn't it?" said Scraggin. "I will charge it to be even more brilliant. It will shine with the light of a thousand stars. When you reach the swamp, throw it as far as you can away from the trail. The swamp rats will swarm to it and you will have time to pass." George nodded feeling relieved. "However, the charge lasts for only two days, so you must return before it loses its strength." George sighed.

Scraggin continued, "The griffin's nest is not far past the swamp. The trail winds through a forest to the base of the cliff. You can leave Nesset under the trees where he will not be seen. The cliff is steep, but not impossible to climb. You will have the mead in a flask and a large bowl. When you win the ledge where the nest sits, pour the mead in the bowl and hide." Scraggin added, "You might call her name to get her attention."

"Right," said George sarcastically. He did not like this plan very much, but he had no other ideas.

Scraggin, noting the unhappy look on George's face suggested, "Why don't you take Nesset out for a walk while I prepare things?"

George agreed, "That's a good idea."

He found Nesset dozing in the sun, which was streaming into the cave opening. He saddled him and mounted. "Let's stretch our legs my friend." They turned up the mountain trail, passing the track to the lake.

It was a lovely day. Thoughts about the challenge ahead faded as George gazed curiously around. It was a rather desolate area. The rocks had taken on fantastical shapes, which seemed to be alive. Beyond them, he could make out ancient gnarled trees that climbed the mountain face.

The peak came into view as he rounded a corner, black and foreboding. It all came back to George in a flash, the griffin and his task. At that moment, he recalled something his father had taught him many years ago. They were hunting and George had shot at a partridge and missed. He was upset and a bit embarrassed. Lord Aaarrun was not concerned, "Next time, think only of what you to want to see." He had counseled. "And when your plans do not turn out as you had hoped, focus on the good in what you have done. This will train your mind to expect the best."

George hadn't fully understood his words, but the following week when he had a wild boar in his sights, he saw the arrow hit the boar and take it down before he even let go of the string. And that is exactly how it turned out.

He decided to use this knowledge now. He imagined himself taking the egg from the griffin's nest, and then handing it to Scraggin. This image gave him more confidence and courage. I can do this, he thought, this is going to work. He turned Nesset and headed back down the trail.

Chapter 14

The Griffin

Scraggin was standing by Nesset when George emerged from the cave. The young knight was dressed in his armor and carried his helmet, weapons and pack. His bedroll, water pouch and a sack of food were already tied to the saddle. George noticed a bag of grain was hanging on one side as well. The ogre, he thought with new found appreciation for the odd little creature.

Earlier, Scraggin had given him the map, a small stoppered pot of the odious salve, the mead, a bowl and the charged crystal. He had also tucked a large sack in his pack saying it was for the egg. "It must be handled carefully. Dragon eggs have thick shells, but they do break, and that would be death to the chick."

They had eaten breakfast in silence. Scraggin set his bowl aside and said seriously, "You are a fine knight. You are clever and resourceful and you learn quickly. I have faith in you!"

George took a deep breath. He appreciated Scraggin's confidence in him. He hoped it would be enough. He wondered briefly how his success might benefit this unusual dragon, but the thought fled as the images of the journey pressed on his mind.

George mounted Nesset and nodded to Scraggin. "Any last words?" he asked grimly.

Scraggin said, "Don't forget that the eye of this dragon is with you." With that, he pulled a gold medallion from under his cloak. In its center shining brightly was a red dragon's eye. It winked. This time George smiled in amazement.

"Ah, there now." said the dragon, "That's more like it!" and he returned a toothy grin.

George and Nesset turned off the main trail to the left onto a narrow track he had not noticed before. It led down the side of the mountain as the map indicated it would. The trail was rough and Nesset had to pick his way among the loose stones.

They reached the beech trees near the floor of the valley as the sun was sinking behind Scraggin's mountain. George made a bed with some ferns, fed Nesset some grain, ate a meal of fruit, cheese and water, then made himself comfortable.

He was tired, mostly due to his anxiety, but before he slept, he thought of Scraggin's medallion, the dragon's eye. And it was red! He shook his head. It must be magic, he concluded. Remembering his own magic trick, he conjured an image of himself carrying the egg back to Scraggin's cave. It felt very real.

George woke with the dawn. He did not pause to eat, but gathered up his bedroll and headed out. Within the hour, they were approaching the swamp. It reeked of rot. He withdrew the crystal from his pack and took it out of the bag. It beamed so brilliantly it hurt his eyes. Urging Nesset closer to the swamp, he could feel his horse's discomfort and murmured reassuringly, "It will be all right, my brave friend."

He stood up in his stirrups, drew back his arm and threw with all his might. The crystal turned in the air like a small star, leaving a trail of sparkling colors, and then fell in the center of the black ooze. George heard the swamp rats surging toward it through the muck. He kicked Nesset into a gallop and they made the far side in safety. Whew, thought George in relief, one down.

They entered the forest, which was covered with a canopy so dense that little daylight could penetrate it. The trail wound to the base of the cliff. George dismounted and tied Nesset to a tree. "You will be safe here. I will return soon." he said with more confidence than he felt.

George unpacked the flask of mead and the bowl. He put them in the egg sack and slung it over one shoulder. Then he opened the pot and, making a face, spread the dark salve on his armor. Scraggin had said to use all of it, but he was overwhelmed with the horrid smell and used only half. "Aggg!" he gagged and threw it into the brush. Then, putting on his helmet, George stepped cautiously from under the protection of the trees and looked up.

His stomach turned over. It was steep and very high. 'Oh, what am I doing here?' He asked himself, but didn't wait to come up with an answer. He reached for handholds in the rock and began climbing. The going was difficult, and he began to sweat as the noon day sun flooded the face of the cliff. George was breathing hard as he pulled himself onto the ledge.

The griffin was sitting on her nest cooing to herself with her eyes half closed. Moving slowly to not make a sound, George took the bowl and flagon out of the sack and set them on the rock. He began pouring the mead into the bowl. Before he could finish, Drugina saw him and screamed. Her shrill sharp cry went right through him. George dropped the flagon and ran to hide in the bushes at the back of the cliff.

The griffin stalked over to the bowl and looked searchingly into the brush. Then she sniffed the mead and drank it noisily. George inched his way over to the nest and climbed in. It was huge! He spied the dragon egg among a collection of odd things, an old shoe, bits of fabric, a large ball of string and many bones. He shivered as he scooped up the egg and put it in the sack. Then he paused to look over the edge of the nest.

Drugina had finished the mead and was still standing! George realized there must not have been enough to put her to sleep. She blinked in his direction and shook her head slowly, then took a wobbly step toward him. George crouched down, his heart beating like a drum inside his helmet. He held his breath. The griffin loomed above him, but her eyes were unfocused. As she raised a huge clawed foot to crush him, George slipped under it and ran to the cliff's edge. He slung the bag over his shoulder and began to climb down.

He slipped and his armor clanged against the rock. The griffin heard it and turned. She made a piercing screech and lumbered out of the nest. Opening her wings, she lifted into the air. George was climbing down as fast as he could, but he realized that he was totally exposed and would not make it to the bottom in time. Drugina swooped down on him and just missed catching his armor with a long talon. She screamed again.

George panicked. He did not want to be another pile of bones in that griffin's nest. He drew the egg around to his chest with one hand, kicked off with his boots and let go. He fell straight down the face of the cliff and landed with a thud on his back. All the air went out of his lungs. As lay there getting his breath back, the griffin landed on the side of the cliff above him, her talons loosened several large stones. George saw them coming and turned over to protect the egg with his body.

A large rock hit his arm and shoulder. The pain was intense. Using his other arm, George dragged himself under the cover of the trees. He laid there for some time. He thought his arm might be broken. Painfully, he sat up and opened the sack. The dragon egg was still whole. He sighed and fell back again.

Chapter 15
The Egg

George had lost consciousness. He jolted awake to Nesset's whinny and then to the pain in his left side. He was stiff and bruised. He crawled to a tree and pulled himself up, then stumbled to where Nesset was tethered. Holding on to the saddle, he said feebly, "I made it back, just like I said I would." He rested his head before mounting. George held the egg in his broken arm and wrapped the fingers of his other hand in Nesset's mane to hang on, then said, "All right my friend, let's go."

It was late afternoon when they reached the edge of the swamp. George could see only a faint glimmer from the crystal. He made out movement on the surface of the ooze. The rats had sensed them. They've probably smelled me too, he thought with disgust. He kicked Nesset into a gallop and pain shot through his shoulder. They raced around the swamp and were still running when they passed the Beech Wood.

George slowed Nesset to a walk as they began the climb up the mountain trail. He halted at a flat place, slid off and sat on a rock. He was exhausted, and Nesset was winded. He could hear the griffin still screaming, and could see her flying over the valley looking for him. George knew he must stay alert. He drank from his water pouch and poured some for his horse in the feed bag. Chewing a piece of dried mutton, he realized he hadn't eaten since the night before. If I can just reach Scraggin, he assured himself through the pain, the wizard will know what to do. He leaned back on the rock holding his injured arm and closed his eyes.

It was near midnight when he opened them again. Nesset had moved closer, screening him from the griffin's gaze. George contemplated the trail ahead and remembered that it was covered with loose stones. It would be unsafe to travel in darkness. He decided to wait until first light before resuming their journey.

"So this is what being a hero is all about, is it?" he said out loud to no one. "Confusion, terror, pain, I just hope it was worth it."

As the pale pink dawn touched the eastern sky, George and Nesset began their weary trek up the mountain. When they had nearly reached Scraggin's path, the ogre ran back to alert the wizard of their approach. George was asleep in the saddle, cradling the egg in his good hand, his broken arm hanging at his side. Nesset was nearly asleep on his feet. Scraggin took the egg and placed it in a waiting basket. He then pulled George onto his shoulder and carried him into the cave. The ogre tended to the horse.

Scraggin set George down on his bench and unbuckled his armor. Then he attempted to pull the chain mail over George's head.

This brought George around and he cried out in pain. Scraggin decided to tend to the arm first. "I see you are injured." he said soothingly, once George had eased off his howling. "I have a poultice to put on the arm and shoulder, and then I will bandage them. I must take off your chain mail and cut the sleeve of your tunic." He explained, "Do you understand?" George nodded and closed his eyes against the pain.

The wizard did as he said and soon George was lying on a stack of pillows with his arm in a sling. Scraggin brought over a cup of hot tea and instructed "Drink this, drink it all, and then rest." George complied and fell into an exhausted slumber.

Many hours later, George became aware of the sound of music. He thought it must be a lute, soft and pleasing. He looked down at his bandaged arm and felt relief and immense appreciation for Scraggin's healing skills, but he was reluctant to move. He allowed the sweet song to lull him back to sleep.

Scraggin was stirring a pot over the fire which woke the young knight. George looked over and saw a large metal bowl sitting on the hearth. In it lay the egg nestled in a bed of straw. This reminded George of the griffin and of his injury. He attempted to move his arm and moaned.

Scraggin turned at the sound. "Ah, you are awake, and I expect you are hungry too." He waddled over to George and helped him to sit up, then brought him a bowl of soup. It tasted of sage and something George could not identify. It was hot and good.

Between sips, George asked, "How did you get me in here?"

"I am a dragon after all," Scraggin replied, "and we dragons are known for our strength."

That seemed to satisfy George. His mind turned to the egg. "Is it all right, the egg?"

Scraggin nodded, "Yes, it is safe and the chick is alive. You did well."

"Drugina," George continued, "will she come looking for it?"

"I don't think so." Scraggin said, "This place is too far from her nest, and besides she knows that dragons rule here."

George drained his bowl and lay back on the pillows. He stared at the ceiling of the cave without seeing it. What he saw in his mind was the griffin's giant foot rising above his head. He closed his eyes and thought I really don't want to see that again, ever!

Scraggin told him to rest and waddled into the next room. A while later, George stood by pushing himself up from the floor with his good arm. He felt unsteady on his feet, but managed to stay upright. He found Scraggin in the workshop stripping herb leaves off of their stalks.

"This is horsetail to make tea." he said to George as he entered. "It will help the bone to mend. I warn you though, it does not taste like peppermint." He looked sideways at George.

The young knight asked, "How long will it take to heal?"

"Are you in a hurry to complete your task?" retorted Scraggin.

George shook his head, "No, it's just that I would like to return to my family before autumn."

"Not to worry." Scraggin assured him. "You have plenty of time to do what is needed, and then you will be on your way." George detected a note of sadness in his voice.

"I will come back." George said quickly. It had come out before he realized what he was saying. He considered his words and feelings for a moment, thinking of the odd dragon here all alone on this wild mountain, and then said again, "I will come back to see you, when I can."

Scraggin murmured something George did not hear.

"What was that?" George asked.

The dragon looked at him intently and said. "Yes, we will meet again. Our

adventures together are not over yet."
The young knight felt befuddled…. again.
"Come, let us brew up this tea." With
that the wizard picked up the basket of
herbs and waddled out.

Chapter 16
The Lesson

When they returned to the front room, the fire had died out. Scraggin gathered some twigs and small branches from a basket on the floor to build another one. He arranged them and then opened his mouth and blew a stream of blue flame into the pile. The tender flared and the dragon carefully laid a log on top.

George exclaimed," Now, that's a good trick!"

Scraggin turned to him, pointed to his blackened nose and grinned, "Back draft." he said.

George laughed, and laughed some more. He fell on the pillows holding his arm. He laughed until tears streamed down his face, washing away the tension and terror of the past few days.

Scraggin giggled with him and sighed. They were quiet for a while. George felt tired again and lay back on the pillows. The wizard gently laid a woolen blanket over him and waddled out toward his garden. The young knight closed his eyes and slept.

What followed was a time of healing and learning for George. He was curious by nature, and he had come to trust the dragon. Scraggin seemed to enjoy the teaching. He read to George from his journal about herbs, healing poultices, and recipes, which all seemed to have something to do with mutton.

He talked of his dragon family. "My sister Hissyp comes to visit at least once a year." Scraggin shared. "She brings me all the news from the clan, chicks that have hatched, who's mating with whom. She loves my mutton pie. Sometimes I think that is the real reason she comes!" he giggled.

George told Scraggin about his family too, about life at the castle and about his friend Lucinda. The dragon nodded at that, but said nothing.

George wanted to know more about magic. He hadn't seen Scraggin actually conjuring, but he was sure the dragon knew a great deal. He was a wizard after all. One morning, he ventured to ask in a conversational tone, "Scraggin, would you teach me some magic?"

"Magic!" the dragon snorted, "and what would you do with that?"

George shrugged, "I don't know, but it seems like it would come in handy. Like the way you charged that crystal to shine like a star?"

Scraggin admitted, "There was some magic to that, true enough. But I have learned the most important thing to understand about magic is that it depends on the ability to focus your mind." He continued, "You must learn to hold your focus long enough on what you want even if you cannot yet see it. If you cannot do that, then no spell or potion will work, or at least not in the way you want it to."

George listened intently. He remembered his vision of returning with the egg. "When I was in the Beech Wood, I imagined myself riding up to you holding the egg. And that is what happened."

Scraggin nodded, "Next time, you might want to put a few more details into your conjuring, like your own safety."

"Yes, that makes sense." George nodded with a grin. "I would like to practice this focus. Will you show me how?"

After a pause, the dragon said, "Fetch that orb from your pack."

George dug it out and then realized, "You knew I had it?"

"I left it for you, didn't I?" replied the wizard patiently.

"So it was your eye that I saw that night in the cave?" George asked quizzically.

Scraggin seemed delighted, "You did get my welcome then! I was hoping you would understand."

George rolled his eyes. He was not about to admit how frightened he was that night.

"Hold it up at eye level," continued the wizard. "Think of a message you would like to send to the ogre. It must have a form."

George thought for several minutes. Then he pictured a sack of grain for Nesset. The image gradually formed in the orb.

Scraggin instructed, "Now hold that image for two full minutes, do not waiver."

George stared into the orb. Other thoughts tried to push their way into his mind but he held them off. Two minutes, just give me two minutes, he thought. There was a noise outside and he went to investigate. A sack of grain sat near the tapestry door. "I did it!" George exclaimed.

"Yes, yes," said Scraggin. 'Now try something a bit more challenging."

"Like giving the egg to Haftnor?" ventured George.

"I do believe it is time to speak of this." said Scraggin. "Come here by the fire. Try these fig cookies while they're still warm."

George sat on his bench and munched on a cookie, "Ummm." he murmured with appreciation.

Scraggin also ate one then began, "In the back of Haftnor's cave is a bed of crystals and precious gems. He tends to it every day. You will wait until he is distracted and then lay the egg on the bed. I want you to stay and watch what he does."

The plan seemed simple enough to George. "You will approach the cave just before dark wearing the black cloak. If you are silent and careful, Haftnor will not detect you."

"All right." said the young knight taking a deep breath.

"You will go tonight."

George started, "So soon?"

"Yes." replied the dragon, "It is time."

As the sun moved toward the western horizon, George moved to the stone bench to put on his armor, which still smelled faintly of the odious salve. Scraggin said, "You will not need that."

"What?" George asked surprised, "Of course I will."

The dragon shook his head, "Your success will depend on invisibility. If Haftnor hears you squeak, or catches the light reflecting off your armor, it will be the end of your quest and of you."

George looked at his armor, and picked up the black dragon shield. The master of the guard had taught him that as long as he had his weapons, he had a chance. He had said, "These are your best offense and defense. A knight's sword and shield are part of who he is. Do not go anywhere without them."

Then George recalled Screemac's parting words to him, "Don't believe all you've been told." George slowly returned to shield to the bench.

"Good." said Scraggin and handed him the black cloak.

Chapter 17
Haftnor

As George put on the cloak, Scraggin brought him a pair of soft boots made from black sheep skin. "And these." he said. George put them on. With the boots, his black tunic and cloak, he appeared to be a shadow. "Perfect!" exclaimed the dragon inspecting him.

Then he carried over the egg which was wrapped in a cloth made with fine golden threads. It reflected the light as if it was on fire. George opened the sack he had used before and Scraggin gently placed in the egg.

"Lay the egg on the bed wrapped in the golden cloth. The light from the crystals will illuminate it which will attract Haftnor's attention, then become invisible and watch what he does."

They went out to George's horse, which was already saddled. The ogre was standing nearby. The young knight mounted, holding the egg in his injured arm. It was bandaged and still ached a bit, but was out of the sling. Taking the reins, he exchanged nods with Scraggin who now wore the golden amulet on the outside of his robe. The red eye looked intently at George, which made him shiver. He turned away and nudged Nesset forward.

Setting off on this journey seemed very different to George. He felt rather naked without his armor and weapons, but also more relaxed and confident. He thought back over all the experiences he had in the weeks since he had left home.

It seemed like it had been a life time. At Scraggin's suggestion, he had spent some time imaging the task of delivering the egg to Haftnor. He had seen himself leaving it on the bed of gems and then melting into the shadows. The wizard had taught him that the skill of invisibility is as important, and can be as useful, as mastering any of the warrior arts. George recognized the truth of this, and was looking forward to testing his new knowledge.

It was twilight when they reached the base of the cave which coned the very peak of the mountain. George left Nesset behind a large stone. He stole up the path until he could just see the opening and could hear Haftnor grumbling. The young knight slipped into the entrance and flattened himself against the wall. The cave was mostly in shadow, but it did not disguise the sight

131

before George's eyes. Now, that is a dragon! He thought.

Haftnor was bent over the crystal bed. He was huge, totally black, and covered with thick scales. Razor ridges ran down his back and ended in a pointed blade on his tail. His immense wings touched the floor. George sensed his power, and his anger.

All of a sudden, this did not seem like such a good idea after all to George. His heart was pounding so loudly he was sure Haftnor would hear it. He wished he had his sword at least. He did his best to be invisible and not to breathe. The massive dragon seemed to be sorting and rearranging the crystals and gems on the large bed. They were beautiful. George saw rubies, diamonds, emeralds and others he could not identify. They glowed with a light of their own.

When Haftnor was satisfied, he moved to the back of the cave. George's eyes followed him. The young knight was astounded to see an arsenal of pikes stacked against the wall. There must be a thousand of them! They were made of saplings with one end narrowed to a point. Haftnor picked up a pike from a pile on the floor and breathed hot flame on the tip to harden it.

This is the threat Scraggin must have been speaking about. Haftnor was preparing an attack! George could make out a few words the dragon was muttering to himself, "Humans, worthless, destroy, mine, mine, mine!"

George took advantage of Haftnor's obsession with his task and stole over to the crystal bed. He carefully took the egg out of the sack and laid it on the gems, leaving it wrapped in the golden cloth. Then his eye caught something else among the stones, a small rusty box with a key hole in it. The image of the key the gnome had given him flashed in his mind. He grabbed the box and retreated silently to hug the wall.

At that point, George thought that Haftnor might wonder where the egg had come from, and that he might look around for whoever had brought it. This realization made the young knight nearly panic. It took all his courage to stand still and not bolt. But Scraggin had said to stay and watch, and the wizard had been right on everything else. So George gritted his teeth and focused on being invisible.

Haftnor finished the pike and leaned it up with the others. He then returned to his bed. His flaming red eyes saw the golden egg. He reached to unwrap the cloth. The black dragon stared at the egg for several long moments without moving. George held his breath until he thought he was going to pass out.

Haftnor then wrapped the egg again, picked it up gently in his clawed hands, walked right past George and out of the cave to the cliff's edge, spread his massive wings and dropped off the side. George could hear his wings beating the air.

The young knight ran out and watched as Haftnor flew toward the east. He could make out only a speck in the gathering dark. Scraggin had been right, the egg was Haftnor's real treasure, and he was gone.

George stood on the cliff, amazed at what he had witnessed. His success and the importance of his part in protecting his people had not yet dawned on him. He just felt relief. He returned to Nesset and whispered, "We did it, my friend." rubbing his horse's head. Before mounting, George looked at the rusty box. He shook it and could tell that there was something inside. I will investigate this later he thought and tucked it in his pack.

The night was clear and full of stars. There was crispness in the air as a full moon rose from behind the griffin's mountain. It reminded George of the harvest, of home and of Lucinda. He smiled at that. He would return as he said he would, and he did have many stories to tell.

The ogre was waiting when George rode up to Scraggin's cave. He took Nesset's reins after the young knight dismounted. The odd creature appeared to be smiling, although George was not sure about that. George took his pack off the saddle and entered through the tapestry door. Scraggin greeted him with a jubilant hug, and George got to experience the strength of a dragon first hand.

Chapter 18

Home

Scraggin had cooked his special mutton pie and plum pudding. "Eat," he said, "and then tell me all about it."

George took a couple bites of the pie. "Delicious!" he exclaimed. The dragon smiled a sight that George had grown fond of.

They finished the meal and George began, "It was as you said it would be, the crystal bed and Haftnor's tending to it. There was also a huge stash of pikes that Haftnor had made. It looked like he was preparing for battle."

"Humm," Scraggin nodded sadly, "it was as I feared. My uncle's anger had consumed him. You came just in time. What else?"

"Well, "continued George, "Haftnor stared at the egg for a long time, and then he just picked it up and flew away." George left out the part about his terror and near bolting. "What will become of the gems?" he wanted to know.

Scraggin smiled, "I have uses for those, not to worry. And the pikes will make good fire wood for the winter. I will send the ogre up to fetch them."

They were quiet for a few moments contemplating the significance of what had happened. Their actions had changed the course of history.

George asked, "Why do you stay here? Why don't you go to live with your clan as well?"

Scraggin replied, "I am rather fond of humans." He waved a clawed hand around the cave. "I like living this way. It is not the way of my family. You saw Haftnor's cave. Let's say I appreciate the creature comforts." he grinned.

"And, in fact, I do watch over your kind. Occasionally, I intervene when they do things that are not so good for them, like damming the river.

"You broke the dam?" George asked in surprise.

"Not exactly, rather I arranged for more water than it could hold." The dragon continued, "And there is another reason I choose to remain here. It has to do with you and our future adventures, which we will discover together. Let that be enough for now. It is late."

George did feel very tired. It had been a long and exciting day. He lay down on the soft pillows, appreciating their comfort, and smiled as he drifted off to sleep.

The next morning, Scraggin was up with the dawn. He had packed George a big sack of food. The ogre had polished the armor until it shown like new. Nesset was saddled and a bag of grain hung from it as well. George yawned and stretched. Now that the challenges were behind him, he felt lighter and eager to return to his family.

They ate porridge and drank tea chatting about the experiences they had shared. George's description of the griffin staggering around made Scraggin laugh.

"Seriously," the dragon said, "you have succeeded where others could not. I am well pleased." This praise felt very good to the young knight.

Then it was time to go. George donned his armor and carried his pack and weapons outside. The ogre was standing next to Nesset stroking his nose, which the big horse had lowered for him to reach. George took the rabbit's foot from around his neck and handed it to the ogre. The little creature grasped it in his hairy hand and stared at George.

Scraggin emerged from the cave wearing his best cloak. It was midnight black with gold stars shining from it.

George felt many things at that moment. Proud of his accomplishments, happy he was returning home alive, grateful to this strange green dragon, and sad to be leaving him.

Scraggin understood all of this. He said, "Be assured my brave young knight, we will see each other again soon. Go now and have a safe journey." Scraggin and the medallion eye both winked. George could not help but smile and mounted.

It was a beautiful late summer day. He and Nesset were half way down the mountain before George realized he had not told Scraggin about the rusty box and the key. He wondered what was in that box and looked forward to finding out.

George rode past the cave where they had weathered the storm. He appreciated even more this day of clear skies and the warm breeze that brought the scent of flowers up from the plains.

He passed through the deserted village and hoped the orphaned children had made it to the castle. Riding between the dragon sentinels, he reflected on how different his experience with dragons had been compared to what he had expected. Not that Haftnor was much different, he thought. He wondered again why these dragons left. He would have to ask Scraggin when he saw him again.

They were making good time. He urged Nesset into a trot and passed quickly through the Tinkling Wood. He sent a silent blessing to those travelers who had become part of it.

A blazing sunset colored the sky as they crossed the river and stopped to camp on the far bank. George laid out his bedroll and opened the sack of food that Scraggin had prepared for him. The young knight appreciated the wizard dragon even more at that moment. He was hungry!

While munching on an apple, George remembered the old box. He took it out of his pack along with the small bag that held the key. He shook the box again, and then he tried the key. It fit, but the lid to the box was rusted shut. George sighed and shook his head. Oh well, he thought, I will take it to the smithy at the castle. He will have the tools to open it.

Thinking of his home and the villagers, he pictured his friend Lucinda, laughing, dancing, and full of life. A feeling of warmth filled him. He tried to imagine his meeting with her, but he found he couldn't. He would just have to let that happen as it did. Smiling, he drifted off to sleep.

The next morning, they stopped at the spring for a refreshing drink and a rest before riding on toward the dark forest. As he turned west, George paused to gaze back at the Black Mountains. So much had happened there. He was aware of how different he felt now. He realized that what he had set out to do at the beginning of the journey had been about impressing and pleasing others. But what he had done was to protect his people from a threat they did not even know existed. And in the process he had learned much about magic and about himself.

George did not meet any gnomes riding through the Stynix Wood, but he did find a bag of acorns with an oak leaf stuck in the top hanging from a branch along the path. He smiled and tucked the little bag in his pack.

It was twilight when he reached the fields around the castle. The farmers and fishermen had all gone home to their families. George rode up to the gate and called to the guard, then waved him to be silent. Entering the castle, the guard was grinning from ear to ear and whispered, "Welcome back, Sir George!"

George returned his greeting in a quiet voice said, "Thank you, Talbot, we will speak later." Another guard walked with him to the court yard and took his horse's reins after the young knight had dismounted. George patted Nesset's head, "We are home, my friend." Nesset whinnied.

The tired young knight took his pack into the great hall. All was still as everyone had gone to bed. "I am home." He whispered, and then thought, this isn't the homecoming I had imagined, but there will be time for celebrating tomorrow. For now, I just want to enjoy this moment. I am so very grateful to be here. With that he quietly climbed the stone steps to his room.

The End

Share in the Adventures of Sir George the Wise Knight and Scraggin Dragon in the next book, The Sea Serpent

About the Author

Valeria Rae worked as a school psychologist for many years and then as a tutor of elementary and middle school age students. She has a passion for medieval history, fantasy and for dragons in particular. Valeria is a freelance writer with many published articles to her credit, and is the author of the Portal Path Inspirational Deck, a set of 52 cards with her original quotes and photography.

Christopher Aaron Barbee has been drawing since he was very young. He specializes in line drawings of cartoons, magical creatures and landscapes.

Made in the USA
San Bernardino, CA
20 April 2017